VIOLET *the* PILOT

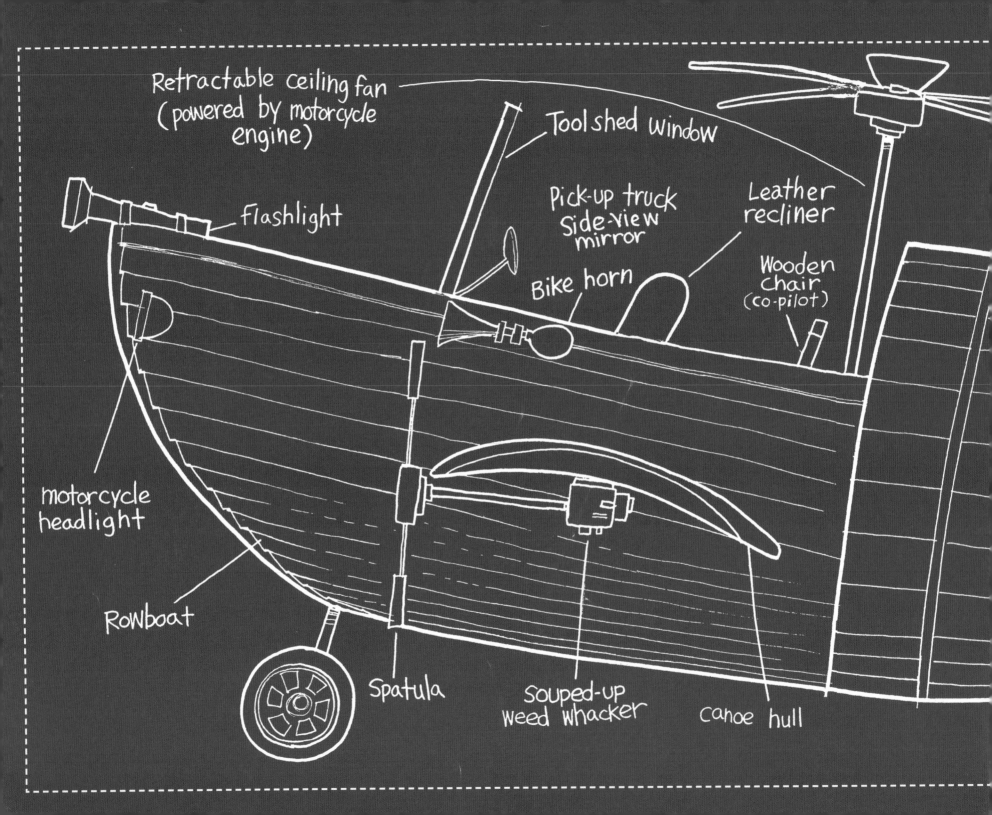

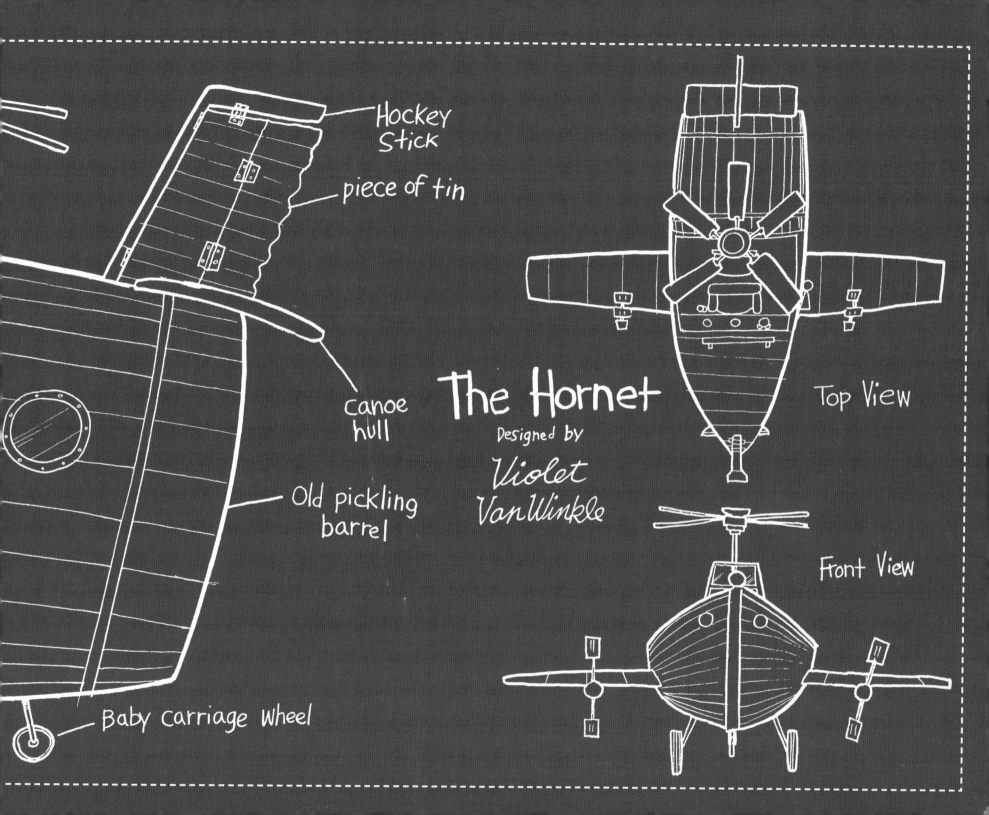

VIOLET the PILOT

Steve Breen

Puffin Books

PUFFIN BOOKS
An imprint of Penguin Random House LLC
375 Hudson Street
New York, New York 10014

First published in the United States of America by Dial Books for Young Readers,
a division of Penguin Young Readers Group, 2008
Published by Puffin Books, an imprint of Penguin Random House LLC, 2016

THE LIBRARY OF CONGRESS HAS CATALOGED THE DIAL BOOKS FOR YOUNG READERS EDITION AS FOLLOWS:
Breen, Steve.
Violet the pilot / Steve Breen.
p. cm.
Summary: Young Violet's only friend is her dog, Orville, until one of her homemade
flying machines takes her to the rescue of a Boy Scout troop in trouble.
ISBN 978-0-8037-3125-7 (hardcover)
[1. Air pilots—Fiction. 2. Aeronautical engineers—Fiction.
3. Popularity—Fiction. 4. Heroes—Fiction.]
I. Title.
PZ7.B4822Vio 2008   [E]—dc22
2007022367

The illustrations for this book were created using watercolor and acrylic paint, colored pencil, and Photoshop.

Puffin Books ISBN 978-0-425-28819-1

Manufactured in China

1 3 5 7 9 10 8 6 4 2

For Jane

Everyone in town knew that Violet Van Winkle was a little different. For starters, she and her parents lived in an odd-looking house next to the junkyard her father managed.

And while other girls were playing with dolls and tea sets, Violet played with monkey wrenches and needle-nose pliers.

Violet was a mechanical genius. By the time she was two, she could fix almost any broken appliance in the house. By four, she could take apart the grandfather clock and completely reassemble it.

Since she didn't have any friends aside from her dog, Orville, she would spend hours tinkering with things from the yard.

Violet's parents were very proud of her (although they weren't too happy the time she put a lawn mower engine on her cousin's tricycle).

The older she got, the more interesting Violet's creations became. Around the time she turned eight, she was building elaborate machines from scratch. And not just any old machines . . .

Flying machines!

Her parents couldn't believe their eyes when they saw Violet zoom by for the first time.

They were a little worried in the beginning, but they quickly saw that she was a pretty good pilot. "Careful not to hit the house!" Violet's father would yell. "And put on a sweater!" her mother would add.

Violet used anything she could find in the junkyard to make her wonderful contraptions.

There was the Tub-bubbler

and the Bicycopter,

the Rocket Can,

the Pogo Plane,

the Slide Glider,

and the Wing-a-ma-jig, to name a few.

Violet's engineering was pretty sound. The only real hazards were tall trees, piles of junk in the yard . . .

and bugs in her teeth.

Kids at school would see Violet eating lunch alone and make fun of her strange books and greasy coveralls. Claude and Clyde Mulrooney were especially obnoxious.

Then one day, Violet noticed a poster in the drugstore window. AIR SHOW OCTOBER 20TH, it read. *That's only two weeks away,* Violet thought. *Can kids fly in the show? Is homemade aircraft allowed?*

That night, Violet sat in her room thinking about the air show. She knew it would be a good feeling if one of her planes won a prize. And maybe then the kids at school would be nice to her. Violet pictured exactly where she would hang her blue ribbon.

She and Orville spent the next few days combing the junkyard for just the right materials. When they had collected a giant pile of stuff . . . the building began.

One day the Mulrooney twins happened to pass by. "Look, it's that girl from school!" one of them said. "What are you doing, weirdo?"

"I'm building an airplane," she told them.

The twins exploded in laughter, then mumbled something mean as they walked away.

Orville barked at the boys, but Violet just went back to her project. "Take it easy, buddy," she said. "We're too busy to worry about them."

Finally, after days of hard work, Violet had finished making her flying machine. She named the magnificent new craft *The Hornet*.

"Wait till the people in the grandstands see me flying *this*!" Violet said to Orville.

The test flight was a success!

On the day of the big air show, Violet took off, bursting with excitement. Her parents' faces had beamed with pride when they wished her luck, and she thought about that as she flew through the clear autumn sky.

She calculated that the trip would take about twenty minutes. She would arrive just in time for the start of the show.

Suddenly, something caught Violet's eye. In the river below, a group of people were waving frantically. Violet lowered her altitude to get a better look. A troop of Boy Scouts had run into trouble while canoeing. Violet knew she had to help . . . fast.

It wasn't easy rescuing all the boys, but Violet piloted *The Hornet* with careful precision.

Saving the scoutmaster from going over the falls was particularly dangerous.

Violet dropped the grateful Scouts off at the hospital,

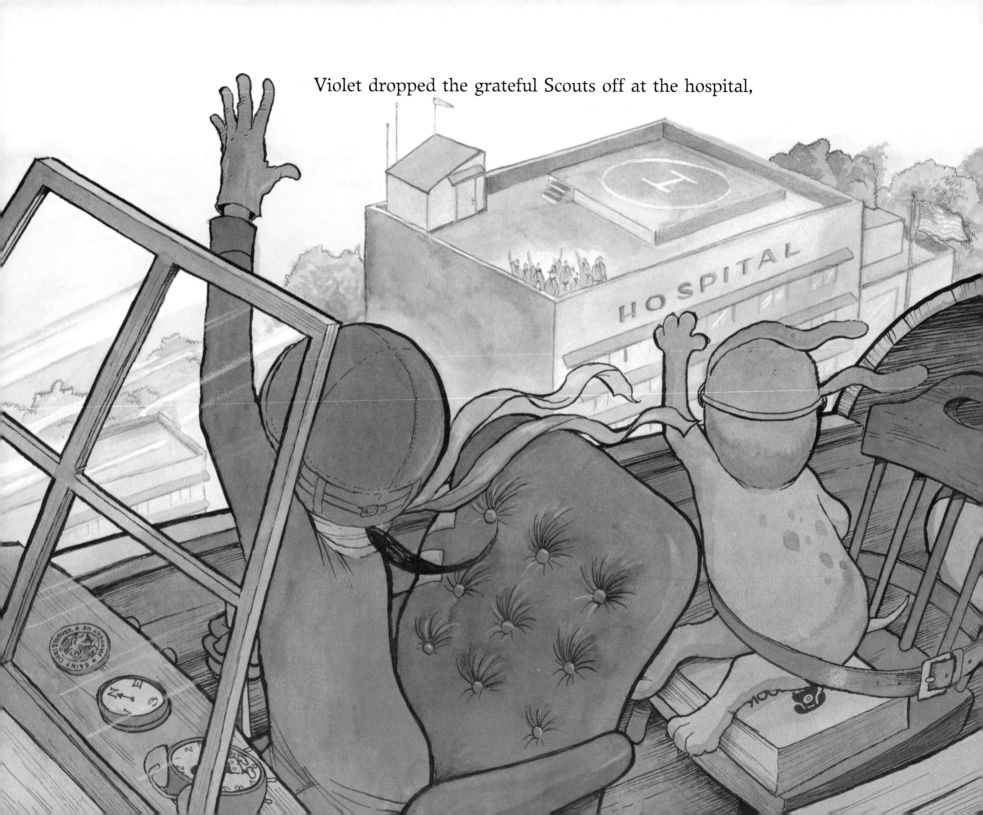

then she checked her watch. "Three thirty," she said to Orville sadly. "We've missed the air show." She turned her plane toward home and sighed. It was a miserable feeling.

That evening, Violet had no appetite for dinner. She just went upstairs and sat on her bed.

All of a sudden, she heard lots of noise outside the house. She and Orville went to the window and discovered that a crowd of people had gathered. Somebody spotted her. "There's Violet!" the boy shouted jubilantly. "THERE'S OUR HERO!"

The Van Winkles stepped outside, squinting from all the flashbulbs that were popping. The press, the mayor, the fire and police chiefs . . . even kids and teachers from school had all learned of the rescue that day and had come to praise her.

"Young lady, please accept this medal of valor as a token of our gratitude and esteem," said the mayor. And he gave Orville a new collar with a license that read K-9 HERO.

From that day on Violet's parents let her fly whenever she wanted.

But her mom still made her wear a sweater.

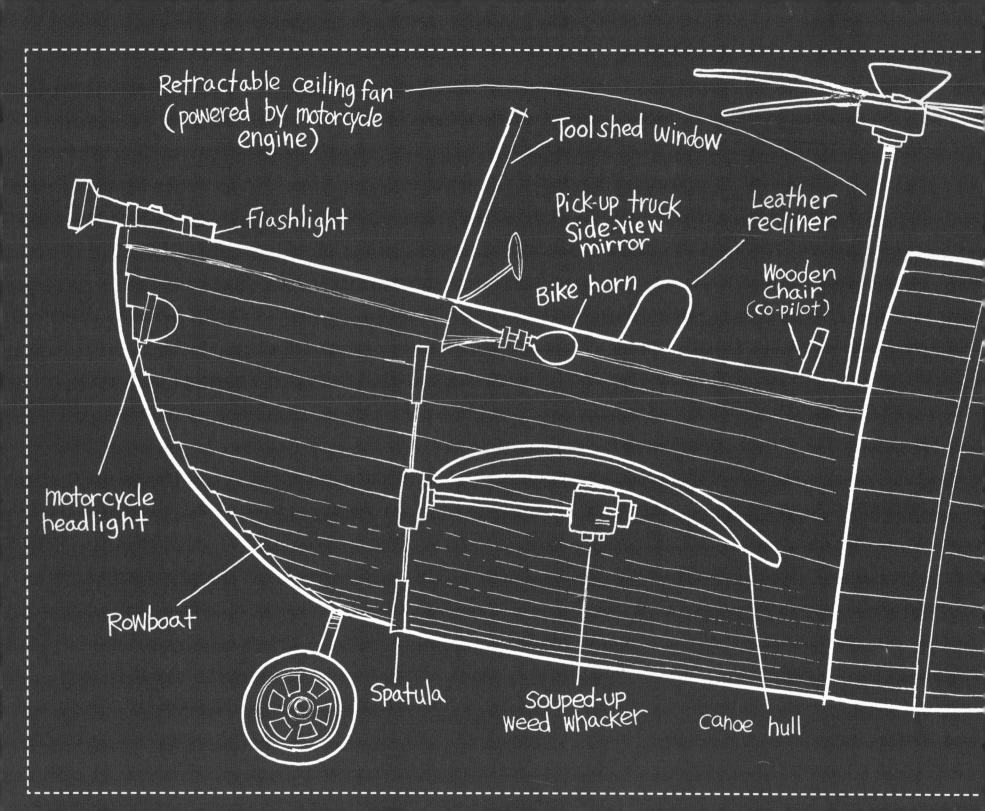

Retractable ceiling fan
(powered by motorcycle
engine)

Toolshed Window

Flashlight

Pick-up truck
Side-view
mirror

Leather
recliner

Bike horn

Wooden
Chair
(co-pilot)

motorcycle
headlight

Rowboat

Spatula

Souped-up
Weed Whacker

Canoe hull

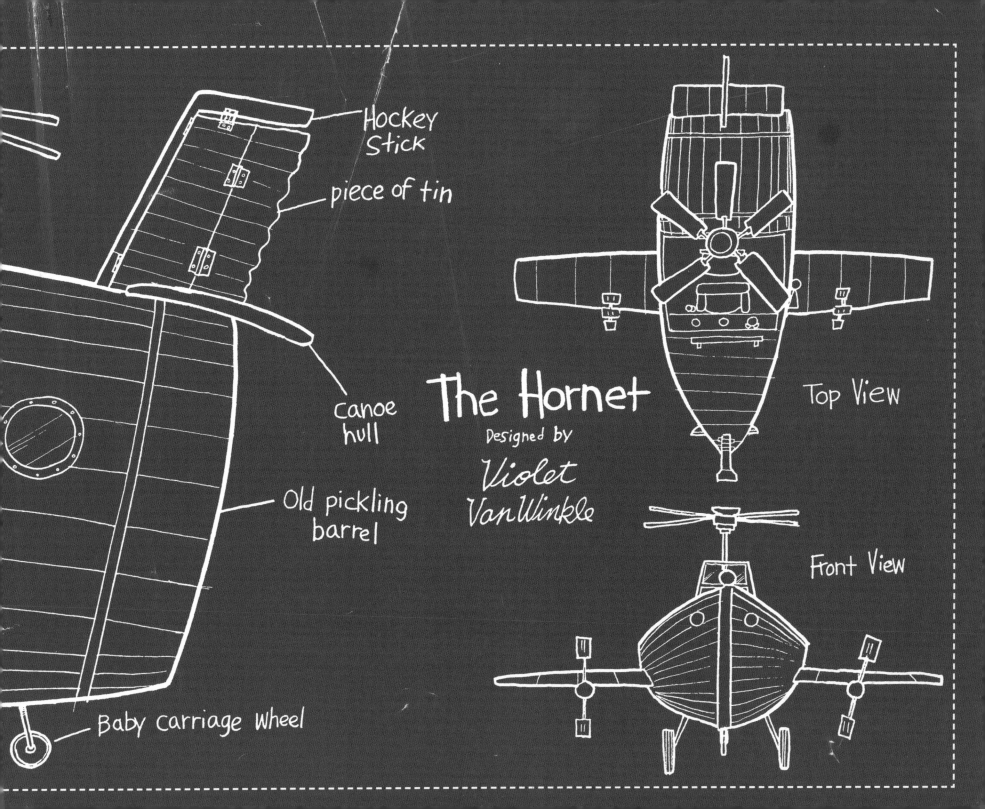

Hockey
Stick

piece of tin

Canoe
hull

Old pickling
barrel

Baby carriage Wheel

The Hornet
Designed by
Violet
VanWinkle

Top View

Front View